Untold Lives

Rema Nair

ISBN: 978-1-67819-901-2

DEDICATION

I dedicate this book to the men in my life, my beloved husband Madhu
Nair and my one and only son Govind.

CONTENTS

ACKNOWLEDGMENTS

My sincere thanks to all my friends and family who have encouraged my creativity.

1   THE FRIEND

Noah and James were out in the backyard. Noah was eight and James, six. They had heard that someone was moving to the house next door. They were curious… would there be kids they could play with? That would be fun!

They were busy kicking around a soccer ball. It was a rough game as they were both very competitive. Each felt very strong and quick and able. So inevitably, there was some pushing and shoving.

As the game progressed, suddenly they heard a noise. The upper balcony of the next-door house overlooking their yard had opened. They stopped their game immediately and watched with interest as an old lady emerged, pulling out a chair and holding a book. She looked over by instinct and seeing the two kids, smiled pleasantly and said: "hello, young men!"

They said hello in return. They were sizing her up, as adults were always people to be carefully evaluated. They were undecided which way their judgment would go… when she asked them their names. Upon hearing they were Noah and James, she laughed in a soft, pleasant way. She said: "That sounds like Nickel and Dime, so maybe I could call you guys that?"

Now James always wanted Noah to make the final call, so unsure, he looked over at his brother. Noah was watching the lady very earnestly. She was looking over, twinkling at them. She had a nice smile and she seemed to want them to accept her… Growling, Noah made the call!

4

"Awrighhht!"

And that was that! They were now Nickel and Dime!

Over the next few weeks, they learned that she lived alone and that she was an avid fan of all their exploits. When they went out into their yard, she invariably showed up on her balcony and she cheered them on in their games, shouting "way to go" or "that showed 'em!" or just plain "awesome!". They felt their egos inflate and their games were a little rougher and when they fell, they were down for a little longer, like some gladiator out for the count. They wanted not just her glowing admiration, they wanted her sympathy and they vied with each other for her attentions.

She had finally been asked to come over for coffee by their mom and they sat in mute respect, smiling happily at her and trying to look all grown up as they politely listened to the conversation. They learned that she was a Mrs.

Bergman, but she insisted she be called Amy. Even by them. Their mother finally talked about how much the kids had come to love her and asked whether she would mind watching them now and then, when she and her husband were busy. They were thrilled! What fun! Now they could talk to her much more, tell her their aspirations, which in their young minds were full of infinite possibilities.

Their first opportunity came the next weekend. They were washed and cleaned and sent over next door while their parents left to meet some friends. Their curiosity was high. They wanted to see her house and assess it for future potential. As a hideout, a stage, a place for their imaginations to take over!

It was a simple house, with plain but cozy furnishings. The living area was large and had an empty space in front of the couch. This will do, for them to act out the tall tales they were planning to tell her. They knew she would listen eagerly and that she was a captive audience.

She learned from them that Nickel wanted to be an astronaut and Dime wanted to be a train driver with a train that can swim. Nickel had heard that in other worlds gravity can make you short and squat or tall and lithe. He wanted to go to a world where he could fly and fight the aliens like a ninja! Dime had heard of the Chunnel and wanted to know why the train couldn't swim.

Nickel did a demonstration of the way he could fly and attack aliens with a sword or spear... with much falling and mayhem, knocking over a small table and some chairs in his excitement. Amy watched him with rapt attention and added in thoughts about the shape and color and might of the aliens to lend more realism to his creations. He was overwhelmed! No adult had ever given his dreams this much importance! He filled his chest and felt like a Superhero!

Not to be outdone, Dime showed off his train, choo-chooing along in a mad rush around the room and occasionally stooping down and pretending to swim as he slithered across the floor. Gratefully, he acknowledged the same worshipping gazes and inclusiveness as his brother. As the hours passed, they were completely enamored by their friend!

Over the next few months, their friendship grew, she got them gifts, toy guns and a train set and so on... they went over to visit frequently, as their parents relied more and more on the sweet old lady. She baked them cookies and cakes and they looked forward to the little treats as much as to her company.

Life was good, school was a bit of a drag, but the evenings and weekends compensated. They gave full rein to their wildest fancies, becoming a firefighter, a pilot, an animal trainer, an actor and a rock star! Each aspiration was received with the same aplomb and encouragement that made them almost a reality. Their lives were full, with many roles to play and many dreams to dream. She made them all possible.

Then one day, there was a knock at their door. Nickel

and Dime were spread-eagled on the living room floor, laboriously working through their homework. Their mother opened the door. It was a cop in his uniform. He wanted to ask her a few questions.

Piqued, the kids sat up, all ears now! The policeman told their mom that Amy was a criminal. She had embezzled from her old job as an accountant with a stockbroker firm. She had been in jail for a while and was out on parole. However, they had never recovered the money from her. She kept denying she had it, although there was ample proof she did indeed. They had traced it back to her in several ways. He wanted to know if she had divulged anything to them. The parole officer had been told of her closeness to them.

Nickel whispered to Dime about hidden treasures they might find at Amy's and they wondered what they would do if they could find it. Maybe give some to their parents, but then also buy the train for Dime or even a small aircraft for Nickel?

Their mom had no knowledge of any of this and convinced of this, the cop took his leave.

But when she turned to talk to them, her disposition had suddenly changed. She was stern. She questioned them in turn if they had seen or heard anything unusual at Amy's. They hadn't. They just played and ran wild and Amy adored them. She never talked much about herself.

When their dad came home later, their parents sat them down and warned them to never have anything to do with Amy again. They were not to go over; she was a criminal and may go to prison again. She could be dangerous. She could have done worse things than that. She was a bad influence! They painted her into a monster to their plastic minds.

For the first time in their young lives, the little boys learned of the limitations of society. For the first time also, they knew the meaning of fear!

*****

2 FOOTPRINTS

Morgan walked home from the bus stop scared and unsure. She had difficulty lately talking to her parents. This time she knew there was trouble ahead, although she didn't know quite what to expect. Her mother and she were the best of friends. But this was way beyond anything she has ever had to deal with. When it came to major issues, her dad had been the ally. But what was he going to say now? She hoped at least he would understand.

All she had told them was that she had something of importance to discuss and needed some time with them. She had given them no hint of what was to come. She simply hadn't known how she could prepare them anyway. A little at a loss, she made her way over the towpath that was a shortcut across the fields to her home.

***

John was home early from work that day. He was a clerk at the little village bank, had been for over three decades and knew everyone well. To the locals, he was their financial adviser, mentor and trustee. His wife Sharon and their eighteen-year old daughter Morgan lived in the little mews house on the outskirts of Aston, a little village in England. With a population of just a few hundred, it was like an extended family estate. Indeed, most families were related by blood or marriage. They were a tight, close-knit and reasonably well-adjusted community. The highlight of their existence was the annual Mayfair when they had neighbouring villagers visit for some fun and games. This was when they showcased their produce, the women's needlework and the local village talent in music and renewed their pride in Aston. He fondly recalled that just last year, their Morgan had been May Queen. He had been so proud.

She had hedged out ole Tim's Lara by a whisker. A not to be put out Tim had insisted he stand drinks for the whole afternoon.

As he drove homewards, the vague feeling of unease returned. The ponderous, uncharacteristic way Morgan had asked for their time seemed to bode nothing good. They had never before been called upon to their parental duty in such a solemn fashion. Morgan was always a good child and had done them proud by going to the nearby town to attend University. She was majoring in British history and English. It had been just nine months since she started. She had found a place to live in - a tiny apartment that she shared with two other young girls, also in school with her. It had been a wrench letting her go, but she came home most weekends and it wasn't far. They could always drive up if they wished, which they did, from time to time.

Last night in bed, Sharon and he had discussed this strange request from Morgan. She had called saying she was coming over to talk to them… Sharon also did not have a clue as to what this could be. Sharon had said there wasn't a boy of particular favour, of that much she was certain. Morgan had wanted to go to London a couple of times, and they had been glad to let her go. They knew she could take care of herself. They had no worries of teenage issues like drugs or alcohol. Besides, she was 18 and they were grateful for the peace of mind and confidence she had given them over the normally troublesome teen years. Sharon had said that all she knew of the London trips were that the girls had simply gone around town, sightseeing and shopping. Try as they might, they were unable to come up with anything that could possibly have resulted in this unusual reaching out for advice from their daughter.

***

Soon he was turning in at the gates to his house and he could see Morgan hanging about the front porch. So, she had gotten here before he could. He looked carefully at her, for any sign as to what was bothering her. She looked anxious, stepping from foot to foot; fidgety was an unusual way for her to be. He parked, alighted, walked over to kiss

her and wished he could still his fluttering heart. She hugged

him, holding on a moment longer than usual, which raised all

kinds of red flags in his mind. His disquiet mounting, he

followed her into the house. Sharon had tea things all ready

in the living room and came in now from the kitchen carrying

hot, buttered scones. Her normally cheerful face was

clouded over with worry, he could tell.

They sat down and tea was poured. Conversation

was stilted, with a forced lightness. Morgan spoke of her

coming examinations and other schoolwork in detail. They

listened, as always marveling at her precociousness. But

neither of them was lighthearted enough to enjoy her

presence, the way she lit up their house. They had always

looked forward to her visits. But this time it was different.

Presently, the tea things were cleared away and

Morgan suggested they all sit down again to talk. They sat

facing her across the coffee table. She took a deep breath

and began:

"Kate, Lisa and I have been doing a good deal of work at school, for what we believe is for a good cause. We feel we have each been given a duty and sometimes we need to do what our hearts tell us to do. We are sure that we can contribute much to what could well make a substantial difference in people's lives. Recently, we had occasion to make such a decision and each of us, independently and collectively, came to the same decision."

This little opening speech was so solemn and portentous that they flinched in their seats and began to imagine what could be coming. Slowly, their hands reached for each other and grasped, holding on to each other in mute solidarity.

"Several months ago," she continued, "we saw in our school magazine an advertisement. It was asking for young, healthy women students who were willing and able, to become surrogate mothers." She paused.

They waited; it had not sunk in yet. Neither of them

understood for a moment what she was talking about. Then Sharon gave a little shriek.

"Oh God, no!" she wailed. "You are not with child? What happened, oh God, please say no!" She was begging her daughter now.

But Morgan shook her head impatiently and went on: "You have to try to understand. This is not like being an unwed mother or something. This is a gift, beyond what you can imagine, to some people who actually see it as a miracle".

All John could still feel was bewilderment. He was too confused to understand fully what she was telling them. Pulling himself together, he plucked up the courage to say:

"Please explain. I am not sure I understand."

"Oh, father!" She turned to him now. "I signed up to become a surrogate mother for a childless couple. I don't know who they are or what they do. All I know is that they are childless and desperately in need of a child of their own."

17

A modicum of understanding was breaking into his senses now. Still, in his unease and chaos, full comprehension continued to elude him.

"Surrogacy! Isn't that where you are on loan for pregnancy?" He asked, hoping he could be wrong.

"Yes" she said simply, dashing his momentary glimmer of hope. "I am not the biological mother; I am just carrying this child for another woman, who is herself incapable of having a child".

In a hollow, deathly voice Sharon was asking: "you mean you have already done this? Or do you mean to do this soon?"

"Yes, mum. This is why we have been going to London those times. It is IVF. It doesn't always work the first time." Finally, her voice faltered. Thus far, she had been resolute and firm, now the little girl in her came through, suddenly unsure and looking afraid. He longed to take her in his arms and chase away her concerns. But reality was hitting him again with brute force. He realized he was afraid himself. Afraid of what he must hear and indeed face over the long term.

Gruffly he urged, "Go on!"

She continued, "It has been 14 weeks now, I have had no problems so far! Not even the customary morning sickness!"

There it was, bald and plain, in their faces. He was struck by a sense of betrayal, of pain so acute that he was beside himself with the agony of it all. He found he was unable to speak. In his numbness, he did not feel Sharon's grip loosen nor see that she had slid off to the side in a dead faint. He just sat there, dimly hearing Morgan's cry as she rose and rushed to her mother. She was coming around, rising back to an upright position now as she held her daughter's shoulders, staring into her eyes.

"Oh God, what have you done, my child!"

They stayed like that for long, tears flowing down their

cheeks, before they hugged each other endlessly, not talking any more, merely sobbing.

Eventually, they broke apart and Morgan went back to her seat. She waited now, waited to hear what they were thinking. Unable to understand his own feelings, he said nothing. Sharon sat huddled, looking broken and diminished, sobbing quietly. Sensing the distress, Morgan rose, saying she was going to her room.

They sat, trying to make sense of how the world had come crashing down in minutes. He could imagine Morgan as a little girl laughing, shouting to be pushed higher and higher as he put her on the swing. Morgan, when she got bullied in school and he had gone to sort out the kid who bullied her, her little glance of pride and confidence as she put her little hand in his; Morgan, as he kept vigil by her bedside while she recovered from a bad bout of the flu;. Morgan's look of radiance and joy as she learned of having been accepted at the university; Morgan as the May Queen.

However, the feeling of betrayal was all-consuming and dominant. He somehow knew Sharon was feeling the same. They had always hoped, had been confident in the belief that their little girl would always have communication open to them, that she knew she had them in her corner. Then why, why had she done this on her own, not giving them the slightest inkling, not asking their opinion?

As the evening wore on, they remained mute and silent, sitting as before, sorting out their emotions, trying to deal with them as they surfaced. They did not talk, did not need to. They acknowledged each other's turmoil without any outward need to demonstrate it.

She was their hope, pride and vision for the future. Sharon had been planning of the wedding they would have for her, John giving her away to a young man who would love and cherish her, of the celebration it would bring to their lives. She was thinking of holding her first grandchild and suddenly it became achingly clear to her that her first grandchild wasn't going to be really hers, wasn't even going to be hers to hold. It had no part of her. She felt defiled and tainted at the thought. As night came on and silence fell in the little village, their home remained dark and still. There was no sign from Morgan's room either. Perhaps she was asleep.

Hours passed and still they sat, each engrossed in thought, dealing with feelings sharp and intense. After a while, John felt his wife slipping into his arms. He held her close, stroking her hair as she clung to him, silent. They stayed together for a long time, till the pale light of dawn lit up the room in a soft glow.

She turned to him then.

"We have always been here for her, we need to be here for her now, also." He stared at her in silence.

Then she rose, her eyes lighting up with life again.

"She made a decision, the first time she made one on her own. It might be right or wrong, I don't think we need be judges of that. Our little girl has grown up. That is all."

He heard her, yet did not. Her words had opened up the wounds again. He struggled anew, with the inner ferment he had quelled to some extent over the hours.

Understanding, Sharon came over to him and softly caressed his aching face. She whispered: "This is not the end of anything. It is just something she felt she had to do. This will be over and done with soon. And we can get on with our lives. We have to help her, she needs care, attention and emotional support while this is going on"

He knew she was right; this was nothing at all. But it was difficult for him. He nodded, still not trusting himself to speak. He knew that when it came right down to it, he would be there for his daughter, would take the lowest blow for her and help and support her in every way he could. It was just that the shock and incomprehension, the sense of betrayal, the difficulty of facing his friends in the village with this, all of which combined to disable him from any thought or action.

Then Morgan was there, looking drawn, her glance

shifting between them as she tried to read their reaction. Sharon was walking toward her, she had aged overnight, looking like an old woman, as she went up to her and took her in her arms.

"My dear, I hope you are feeling alright," she said.

Hugging her tightly back, Morgan was murmuring, "thank you" over and over. As he watched the two women in his life, John suddenly felt his pain, fear and doubt evaporate. They would do this together and with luck, it would all go well.

His shoulders square, his jaw set, he came to a definite decision. He had made up his mind. He held out his arms. He had to face it. His little girl had grown!

*****

3 ABSOLUTION

She had wept until her eyes burned, when, as a bride, she was led to the car that would take her away from her parents and childhood home. Her sisters also had broken down with the sudden realization of the parting that they had forgotten about in the midst of all the revelry of the wedding celebrations.

As she drove away with the stranger who was now her husband, she was forlorn. Barely out of her teens, she had never yet known a life that was outside her immediate family. Gently, he had reached out and taken her hand. He had given her a reassuring squeeze and she suddenly found herself gripping his hand with all the fervor of clutching at a straw. And, inexplicably, a bond was formed. A bond that had never taken hold until that instant, not through all the sacred wedding rituals they had undergone together and the tacit vows that they had made to each other through the various ceremonial activities.

Over the next few days, she found herself drawn to him, as she learned the ways of her new life. He was kind, patient and strong. He eased her into life with his family, in a city far away from home and she fell into a new routine of happiness and love.

Then it had come, the transfer to Kashmir. Her husband, who was a Major in the Indian army, was deployed in the mountainous state for possible action in the war zone. He tried to dissuade her from going with him, but she was adamant, she needed to be by his side, she couldn't bear the thought of him so far away and in the midst of extreme danger while she spent her days in fear. She insisted on going.

They had travelled there, a long journey by train, her anxieties rising over the potential dangers of her beloved's assignment. As they pulled in to the Srinagar Station, they had seen heavily armed commandos, guarding every exit and watching everyone closely. They had to pass through multiple checkpoints, before finally getting into their taxi for the army base, where they were to have their quarters.

They had settled in once again to a new life. His days were regimented, he could come home for lunch and he was back again by 6 pm, so they had their evenings to get together with fellow army folks or explore the breathtaking beauty of the Kashmir landscape. He was not at the warfront; he just had normal days in the safety of the army base. She spent her days cooking, although they had army personnel to take care of them. She loved to cook for him and watch him relish her lovingly created, but not very expert attempts at variety.

Despite all the tensions in the area, those were peaceful days and their life together was serene and full of love. She adorned herself with flowers form Gulmarg, the meadow of flowers that was famous in Kashmir… awaiting his arrival in the evenings. Then they spent hours in blissful togetherness, not a care in their immediate lives, as the months flew by.

Then one evening, he was coming back early from work and had called ahead to inform her. Having decided to surprise him, she had walked over to the entrance, sitting on the bench nearby, in pleasurable anticipation. Soon, his jeep had turned into the street outside and her heart was leaping with joy. She stood up, waiting for him to see her and delight as his face lit up with surprise. All too soon things changed… as if from nowhere, she noticed another car coming around the corner towards his in great speed. It seemed headed straight for his Jeep; they were on a collision course… she felt a screaming in her nerves as she strained to see, praying for the moment to pass…

Inevitably, there came the huge crash and a terrifying boom! Her soul cried out as if it would tear out of her body in a fiery wail. She could smell the burning air and the smoke was so thick she could not see anything at all. Presently, the air cleared and she began to see through the smog. There was just twisted metal and rubber, fragments scattered for yards around the two main lumps. She tried to run towards the heap, but suddenly there were people reaching for her, holding her back while she struggled and squirmed in vain.

***

Soon, she went back to her parents. She had nowhere else to go. As she arrived, she saw the helplessness in her father's eyes. Her mother reached for her and hugged her, never saying a word. It had been a long while since she had left her sisters, though they still behaved as if she had never been gone. But she was oddly unmoved by any of them, they seemed like strangers to her. She moved into her old room and tried to stay away from everyone, as much as she could.

Over the days and months that followed, she

developed a crusty shell around her, shielding herself from the pain and nostalgia that never really went away. She went through the motions, eating what she could, sleeping a lot, never venturing to do anything more than was required of her. She largely ignored her siblings' inane attempts to include her in their ventures. A settled gloom was her constant companion.

A few years of indifference passed and she still continued in her studied moroseness, although even she could not fail to note the despair and some impatience that she often felt from her parents. One day, they had sat her down and told her about their own incapacities as they grew older and how they were concerned about her life. They had two other daughters to marry off and were worried and clueless about what would happen to her. She had a small pension that was due to her from her husband's passing. It was adequate for her immediate needs, but it only served to detract from forcing her to try to find any purpose to her life. Her formal education had not gone beyond high school and she had no real skills that were apparent. They felt she should try to learn some art or handicraft, do something productive, that she could take comfort from. She was jolted into an awareness for the first time, by their valid concerns and by the cold reality of the burden she had become to them.

After the talk, she went back to her apathy, but there was a nagging in her now that she was a source of concern in the household. Eventually her sisters were married and left the home. Over the years she changed, her features coarsening, a few strands of grey running through her thick, black hair. The few months that had been married life for her were becoming a distant memory, something that she still cherished, but was losing in clarity in her mind.

The lethargy had settled upon her as a shielding cloak. It had become her nature, her predisposition. General apathy and doing nothing had become her habit. A venture of any kind had become alien to her.

***

Over a decade had passed when one evening, in her customary fashion, after she had retreated to the haven of her room, she heard her father call out to her. Disinterested, she made her way out to the living room. A stranger, a young boy stood there. He was fair-skinned, tall and lanky, wearing the long tunic and fez cap of a typical Kashmiri youth. Memories came to her in a rush. People and places long forgotten were flashing across her mind. Piqued, she greeted him.

He stood there, his hands folded in the traditional greeting, gazing at her in a deep, gentle way. Suddenly interested, she asked him: "Who are you?"

He seemed a little hesitant to start, and then tentatively said: "It may be a little painful for you to hear, but I am someone who has been trying to find you for a while now". He went on to say that he was the son of the suicide bomber who had been responsible for the bombing that had killed her husband. His father was a rebel Kashmiri, fighting for a separate homeland. He was merely a child at the time, and had not known a lot about his father's death, except that he was a hero in his neighborhood.

Listening to him, she felt repulsed. Searing anger was consuming her. Unable to react to it, she stood there, her attention focused for the first time in years! He continued, still standing. No one in the room would offer him a seat.

He had grown up in the little village in Kashmir, the son of a hero, with all the honor and respect of his neighbors and friends. His mother, now a widow, had taken pains with her two young children, giving them all the love and encouragement they needed as they grew older. He had heard the tales of his father's glorious demise many times, which suggested that he had died fighting the enemy in combat. With the gentle shielding of his mother, he never knew who the enemy was or much of the painful political details of the unfortunate state of Kashmir. Theirs was a simple, rustic life; led by their mother, whose feminine ways provided a gentle and tender upbringing for them. She herself was not involved in the public life too much, their little home mostly of an agricultural and farm type, where they tended sheep and grew their own vegetables. Finishing school, feeling responsible for his family, he had quietly gone to Srinagar to enlist in the army.

That was when he had had the shock of his life. He was confronted by an officer who had questioned him at length as to his motives for joining the forces. He was confused and rattled by the hostility of the interrogation. Then, slowly, it had all started to sink in. His father had been a terrorist, someone who had killed himself and a Major in the Indian army in a horrific, stealthy, suicide attack. He was not eligible to enlist and was actually being treated like a suspect.

Over the course of the questioning, he had begun to realize that his hero was not a hero at all, but someone who had actually murdered an innocent man returning to his home. His sensibilities had been overturned in practically an instant. He found growing in him a deep sense of shame. Defeated and appalled, he had made his way back home.

He had reflected on his new reality for a number of days, before he found the courage to confront his mother. She had listened to his tale, of how he had gone to the city to find himself a job in the army, in what he thought was his father's footsteps! At first, she had tried to silence him and deny the truth of it. Then over the days, she had found that she had to acknowledge his concerns.

She herself had not known a lot of the details of her husband's activities. He used to disappear, sometimes for days at a time, and she had merely gone on with her life. When he had been home, they were happy. She had never probed too much into his affairs; men will be men, after all! As she thought about it all, she began to realize that her son may well be right after all.

When he had died, all she had known was that his death was glorious and heroic and she had taken comfort from the fact and moved on with her life. Her children and her little farm had occupied her life.

Overall, she was a devout woman, simple in her logic, but deeply philosophical and kind. At first, however, she had refused to believe, and initially totally rejected her son's tale. But she was deeply disturbed by his details. She had searched in her mind for some answer, for she loved her boy deeply and wanted to give him peace. A few weeks passed before she had finally asked him about the man who was killed. He did not know a lot, but he had been a Major in the army and was returning home to his family, when he was killed. She found herself thinking of the family then. The loss they must have felt! What were they like? She had sent her son back to Srinagar to find out.

***

Having concluded his tale, he stood before her, watching her closely for a reaction. His mother had asked him to track her down and offer her her deepest sympathies.

He informed her of their sorrow at learning their own truth and how ashamed they had become of it. Their apologies were inadequate, he said, but they were contrite all the same.

Having said that, he said he would be back tomorrow to talk to her again, he was staying in the lodge nearby. She wanted to tell him not to come back, but then something held her back... maybe she wanted to see him again...

He was back in the morning the next day and this time she asked him to sit down and offered him tea and snacks. Tentatively at first, then with a slow animation, she questioned him about his home, his life, his land that had been so much a part of her own happiness. She drank in his tales and felt a stirring of animation that was so foreign to her. She asked him to stay a little longer, spend a week at least, in her town. He did not refuse. He visited often and they became unlikely friends. They were warm and close to each other, falling into an easy conviviality that was very comforting to each. It was on the penultimate day of his stay that he finally broached the subject to her – would she consider going with him to visit his mother? She would be so happy to see her!

She was alarmed at first, but the thought gripped her almost immediately, the thought of visiting the land of her dreams. Her family was initially skeptical, then happy that she was doing something for herself. They helped her to pack and he arranged their travel. That night, she went to bed eager for the next day. She slept deeply with a comfort she had not known in a long time.

***

Her visit to Kashmir was a success. In the instant they met, the two women, long starved of any sense of kinship, had formed a strong connection to each other. They had both endured, in their own respective fashions, the vagaries of life that had been theirs through no fault of their own. They each felt a profound sense of affinity for the other in their shared misfortune. Their attachment was immediate and their initial days together crystallized and solidified the relationship. She also reveled in the beautiful land that had been the backdrop of her nuptial happiness. She found herself a willing participant in the daily running of the farm. Her departure was never spoken of and the days extended to weeks and then months. The carapace that she had created around herself, her crustiness, slowly fell away and she found herself in a state of complete contentment.

Weeks turned into months and then years and nobody ever even thought of her return to her home. She had become a part of the household, a sister to the mother, a loving aunt to the kids, their lives her own. Life was good, her purpose had been found.

*****

4 A BEATING HEART

He was a young man in his mid-twenties. Life had always been good for him. Born into an old and affluent family, he had had a childhood full of affection, with all the attentions of doting parents and grandparents. He was a bright kid, good at his schoolwork as well as soccer, hockey and amateur dramatics – all of which gave him a well-rounded upbringing.

Now, in the prime of his youth, he was full of promise and assurance. Everything boded well for him. There were no clouds on the horizon. Life was good.

And it was on one Friday evening when he had gone to meet friends that, what with one thing and another, they ended up staying late. They had had a few beers and it was past midnight when the jolly party finally wound up and one by one, they started to leave. He was usually one of the last ones and draining his glass and signaling to the bartender to adjust his tab, he headed out.

The area was one of the more happening places in town and there were bars and restaurants dotted around, with bright lights and music coming from various directions. It was the Fort Lauderdale area and he only had a short walk to his home.

He had barely walked a few paces when out of the darkness came a woman. She was slight and wispy, but she careened full into him, so that he reeled. He reached out to clutch her as he fell and she fell on top of him. Dazed for a moment, he finally focused on his new companion. And the breath went out of his lungs. For he was staring at the most beautiful face he had ever seen.

Her eyes were wide and beautiful, her oval face so perfectly proportioned with a crescent shaped brow and sweet, full lips. He now realized that she was just a slip of a girl, not quite a woman. Her hands as she held him were thin and long. Her hair was straight and long, but full. In the light, she looked small and vulnerable. And breathtaking!

If there was love at first sight, then that was what happened to him. Instantly, he was captivated. He could not breathe lest the moment was lost. He just stared mutely at the girl.

They must have stayed that way for a while, for it was she who broke the spell. Murmuring her apologies, she stood up and held out her hand. He noticed that she was neatly dressed, though only in a teenage fashion. Not quite in adult clothes. They hung loosely on her. She was smiling now, her eyes lighting up. He felt his heart give a little leap!

He reached out and grasped the extended hand and pulled himself up. It all felt somehow unreal to him. He let out his breath and tried to stop from staring at her. Affecting nonchalance, he asked her if she was alright.

***

All of that was a few weeks ago. He had, of course, asked her her name and offered to walk her home. She was living a little farther away, in a little house slightly off the beaten path. It was definitely not in his usual area. He had taken her home and at her doorstep, asked if he could see her again.

They had been meeting for weeks when he started noticing some things about her. Although she was always clean and even smartly dressed, she didn't seem to have too much of anything. Also, she sometimes went all incommunicative. There were times when she just stared into space and did not seem to hear him at all. He thought there was something bothering her, but he had the feeling he could not ask, that it would not be welcome. She just stared into space and looked so lovely, like a Modigliani painting, that he was content to just let her be.

He knew that she showed no hesitation in wanting to be with him and always came to him when he asked. She was even enthusiastic in her quiet and reserved way. As they spent more and more time together, he felt that

someday, somehow, he will know what was the matter with

her. For the moment, he was content to just let her be and to

share those evenings and weekends, all infused with an

endless charm, a strange inner glow of warmth.

***

Things would have gone on this way for a while, had

not something happened one night. It was just another

evening when they hung out and went out to the beach

again, for the umpteenth time. In the pale moonlight, she had

an ethereal quality about her which made him catch his

breath again. They walked arm in arm aimlessly, just talking.

Rather, he was talking. About his dreams and his work and

what he was hoping to achieve, in the next couple of years.

He had a lot to say about all of that, his days were always

full.

Suddenly, she flung herself to the ground and when

he looked down at her, he saw that she was shaking. He

dropped instantly beside her, reaching for her to hold her

close. She continued to shiver uncontrollably in his arms. And then, just as suddenly, she stiffened and seemed to have passed out. He held her close, but he was feeling completely lost. He looked around and could see no one who could help.

He reached for his cellphone and dialed 911.

In moments, the paramedics arrived and she was being taken to the hospital. He knew only her name and where she lived. Surprisingly, he did not have many more details to offer.

Sitting in the ambulance next to her, he felt completely miserable. Had she had some type of seizure? He stayed as they took her into the emergency ward and later, when they had more tests to do, they asked him about her family. He did not know. They enquired at the address and discovered that it was a rooming house and she had been living there for a few months.

He learned that she was barely eighteen and that she

was suffering from opioid misuse. How strange it was that he had never seen the signs! Or maybe, he didn't want to see.

He stood around while they made her comfortable and helped her in every way they could. It was morning when he finally went home.

When they finally let her go, there was no reason to keep her, he was there. He helped her get to her home and offered to get her anything she wanted.

But she was, once again, mute and stubborn. She merely shook her head at everything and indicated that he should leave. In despair, he turned around and left.

Over the next few days, he tried to see her and help her as much as he could. But she was not responsive and merely stared, seemingly not even knowing he was there. He knew that she was getting her drugs, but he did not know how and when.

Then, one day, things got out of hand. He had just gone up to see her when she suddenly turned on him and taking a pan from her little kitchenette, she swung at him and hit him wildly on his shoulder. Startled, he turned when she swung at him again. This time the blow hit him on the side of the head. She was suddenly screaming at him to go away. She never wanted to see him again.

She was advancing on him again when he turned to leave. Tears were pouring down his face now. But he knew he had to leave. This was not something he could comprehend. It was an ugliness that broke the spell for him. The tears were flowing for the love that was dead. This time he knew he would never come back. Sometimes, the head has to rule the heart.

As he left, he did not see her face as she turned away, or the sadness written on it, as she let him go.

*****

5 THE LITTLE MASTER

It was a plan that had been taking shape in his mind ever since he found the parchment at a pawnshop on one of Alexandria's little side-streets. He had gone into the shop looking for a deal as he had heard lots of stories, of true antiques that might be found, fortunes to be had, if one cared to look hard enough, in the little shops of Egypt. And all for a song! He assumed that at least some of the tales were apocryphal, but he knew that for these stories to gain credence, there must be a grain of truth in the background.

He had scoured the little touristy places and gazed greedily at the objects on display, well outside his budget. Little scarabs and clay signs, seals and tablets priced way over anything he could afford to buy. Disheartened, he had

taken to scouting the less frequented neighborhoods, setting

out each morning, fresh coffee in his belly and even fresher

hope in his heart. But, as the days wore on, his vacation

slowly coming to an end, his spirits sank lower and lower.

Until the very last afternoon of his vacation, when,

worn out from the day's wanderings, he came upon a little

shop that had just a door and no façade. There was only a

lopsided little board atop the door that proclaimed its status

as a shop; it seemed to say knick-knacks, from what he

could understand by sign-reading Arabic as he had learned

to do. It was dark and uninviting to the passer-by. But he had

nothing to lose and a few minutes respite from the sun

seemed like a good idea.

Walking in, he found a young man inside, showing

signs of the ennui that must have been a part of his life, if

this was indeed his vocation. He barely looked up and did

not acknowledge his presence. He seemed to be doodling

on a worn writing pad with an even more tired pen. Ignoring

him, Chang walked over to the little showcases with the items for sale inside. It was difficult to see the display as the lighting inside was poor. He saw some sad looking copies of hieroglyphics, a few mud ewers that were allegedly used for storing alcohol a long time ago, their ears and lips cracked and their sides chipped. Unimpressed, he moved on and then he saw them. Old sheets of what appeared to be parchment, that looked like they had nothing written on them. Intrigued, he finally turned to the young man and made a noise in his throat, trying to draw his attention.

Reluctantly, the man had gotten up from his desk and ambled over. Chang had then pointed at the sheets. The man had broken out into a rush of speech, of which the only word Chang understood was 'canvas'. Indicating with a motion of his hand, he had enquired its price. 20 piastres for a sheet. That had seemed like nothing at all, finally, to Chang. On impulse, not because he saw any need for it, he had bought one sheet of canvas that the man rolled up in a newspaper for him to take away.

It had been safely lodged among his things as he took the flight back home to Guangzhou. Arriving back home, Chang had fallen back into his routine of working for the toy factory, painting little wooden toys with bright colors in endless monotony. There was no creativity, he merely had to follow instructions and slap on paint as directed.

Poor Chang, he fancied himself as an artist, had trained for years under Master Bao, hoping for recognition and at least an art director's job at any of the multiple factories that seemed to spring up everywhere with the new economic revolution in China. But getting good breaks was not easy, with most of the urban population looking for employment in mass production jobs. He had taken to working at the toy factory in order to meet his living needs, but had never given up the dream of making it big one day.

As the years passed, he had lost more and more of his optimism and was becoming resigned to his mediocre fate. It was in a moment of wild adventure that he had gone to Egypt, using much of his savings in a vain hope of rekindling his fate and having an adventure.

Returning from the trip, he was disappointed and regretted the mad impulse of going. As he fell back into his humdrum existence, his evenings began to beckon to him more and more. He fell into the habit of dreaming a fantasy world for himself where everything was possible and he was a master artist, liked and admired by all.

In his dreams, his creations took on all aspects of meaning; they were masterpieces, each unique and capturing the imagination of all who could view them. In his visions, he created the most magical versions of art, paints with hues, shapes and texture that no one had ever imagined before. He knew he had it in him. The talent of a Ming dynasty craftsman or a Sandro Botticelli! It was in one of these grandiose flights of fantasy that an idea started germinating. Gradually it took shape, form and direction. Finally, it solidified into a plan to create a fake masterpiece on the old parchment from Egypt and to be able to sell it at a premium to one of the top galleries in Guangzhou, so that he could make enough to start his own art studio.

Suddenly obsessed, he took to working on the details of the ambitious plan. Feverishly, he researched online, from the little internet café in the corner, about the ways to age a painting artificially. He avidly studied the mediums and the way time affected them. He learned of the way grime would stick to dull the colors and laboriously outlined the delicate ways he could detail the ageing on paint. He wrote out his game plan in painful detail and ironed out each kink as he ran into it. He realized from the start that he would have to use oil. Tempera had been widely used in medieval times, but he was not sure he could age the organic pigments in a convincing way. Tempera colors never faded and they couldn't be applied in thick layers as oils could, nor did they have the deep color saturation that oils had. Oils become dark, yellow and transparent with age and he was confident he could strive to achieve a similar effect with some hard work and lots of skill. Besides, oil paintings were only a few centuries old and he hoped to use only mineral pigments that would throw off all carbon dating attempts without any precision. He had to use an oil medium and decided to use the oldest oil he could find at his grandmother's. He hoped this would be at least a few decades old and its chemistry would be hidden by the mineral pigments that were simply timeless.

Soon, however, he hit a snag. Canvas was not a usual base for old masterpieces. And in China they had used silk. His little sheet of canvas would be woefully inadequate. He decided he would create a painting in the style of the Masters on the canvas regardless. He hoped he could be convincing if he tried something original. But as he started his work, he realized that seal brown had to be the color of choice and should be used as the base for his work. It added authenticity.

He had decided to paint a little portrait of a lady, much in the likeness of the little Chinese princesses from the 15th century. Once his plan was meticulously outlined, he had set to work in a frenzy, each evening, rushing home from the toy shop to actualize his dream. Slowly, the picture had taken shape and form and color. He was careful, painstaking, sparing no little detail that he felt could add to his achieving the desired dullness of age and beauty it must acquire in order for him to be able to pass it off as a grand old treasure.

For weeks he toiled on it, forgetting to eat and sleep as he saw visions of a new life rising with each stroke. The little princess was charming, ethereal and almost unworldly as Chang strove to make the picture yellow and transparent. It took on a life of its own as Chang gazed at it and even he could see that it was ineffably beautiful and imbued with an arresting quality. He had used fine films of acid and base to achieve the ageing, depending on the pigment chemistry. He had stroked on the flimsiest layers of dust and grit in an effort to create the patina of age. The background of the picture offset the princess in the palace gardens. He attended to every little detail, like a fond parent. Every plant, leaf and flower received the most reverent attention. He was finding a fulfillment he had never known in years of toil at the toy factory.

Finally it was done. He took days, putting in finishing touches, a dab here, a scrub there. Drinking in the details, assessing with a critical eye and perfecting it, bit by bit, in the tiniest particular, he found himself slowly marveling at his own handiwork.

***

He was spent and decided he had to dispense with the possessiveness he felt over his creation if he were to move his plan forward. He needed validation, his work had to be adored and worshipped by all. To revel in the pride and glory that would be his when he unveiled his masterpiece.

Carefully putting away his canvas into a wooden frame, he dressed fastidiously and in a burst of euphoric extravagance, took a cab to the Chi Shen, an art gallery and auction house, a world-renowned purveyor of the finest and the best that he knew would offer the most fitting home for his grandiloquence. Arriving at its hallowed portals, Chang alighted from the taxi and made his way in with an assumed confidence that he did not feel.

The reception was all oak paneled and elegant with a ceiling so high that it made him dizzy gazing upwards. A young woman with the delicacy of a fawn, was at the counter. Intimidated, he approached, trying in vain to feign nonchalance. The vision at the desk asked, in a demure, hushed tone:

"And how may we assist you?"

Awed, Chang started to stutter...

"I... I mmmight have sommmething of interest, a fffffamily heirloommmmm!" He waved ineffectually at his parcel.

The being now deigned to cast a glance at his flailing

arms.

"I see! You might need to see Mr. Shi, but he only cares to see the very best of the best! Please enlighten me, what do you think you have in there?"

This was the moment of truth. Mustering all his courage, he slowly took his canvas out of the wrapping.

"It is an early Ming dynasty relic my ancestors left me! It is priceless!" he exclaimed. Trying hard to still his fingers, he slowly drew out the picture. Trembling, he unfurled his magnum opus in front of its very first viewer. It opened, like a spring flower, like the dawn of a summer morning before her overawed gaze. Chang heard her sharp intake of breath, a sibilant hiss and he knew he had her. Without a word, she arose and was gone, into what unseen presence, he did not know.

Presently, he was ushered in to Mr. Shi's office. Rendered almost speechless with reverence, Chang was bowing and curtseying in absolute devotion at the sight of the man the world venerated, whose most flippant statement could make or break an artist's life. Soon, he was explaining his treasure, a family heirloom, handed down for generations, from the time of the Ming dynasty. Soon he was laying it out before Mr. Shi's eyes. He was a portly man, dressed immaculately in a beautiful suit, chinless and hairless, like a Mandarin. He stared, deep and long at the portrait, silence reigning in the room.

Before long, he started, as from a reverie. Turning to him, he said:

"Mr. Chen, we will have this piece evaluated and let you know its worth. If we may, we will retain it for further appraisals. Please leave your name and address on your way out!"

Chang could only nod mutely and follow the receptionist out. His baby, the little painting he had come to hold dearer than his life, was now in its ultimate test of truth.

***

A few weeks passed before he got the call. Mr. Shi would like to see him. In trepidation, he arrived back in his presence at the appointed time.

Mr. Shi was affable. He offered him a seat and handed him a fine plum wine. Once he was settled, he got to the business on hand forthwith.

"Mr. Chen, we have a buyer for your piece of art. He has offered 80,000 Yuan for it. We are pleased to make this offer to you on his behalf."

Chang felt a sinking sensation. He had been hoping for ten times this offer at least. This was good, but by no means stellar. It would help him a long way, but will by no means realize his dreams. He felt the offer belittled his efforts and the passion of his creativity. He shook his head. His stutter was back.

" I… I ccccannnot accccccept! This is a treasure. Yyyyou are trying tttto rob mmmme!" He was losing it now.

"Mr. Chen, calm down! We Chinese are an old and

ancient civilization." said Mr. Shi. "We invented paper! In 200

BC! We never needed canvas, certainly not in the period of

the Ming dynasty, circa 15th century AD. We also invented

silk. We like to paint on silk. It is a fine and regal fabric. You

are very talented. But you need to be more careful. This is a

most beautiful work of art and certainly, it is fetching a most

generous price. Mr. Chen, don't lose heart yet. We have a

proposition for you. If I may, I think we have a winning

strategy here…There is a potential market for your unique

and obviously winning art form. If you insist, we could import

canvas or, even better, use canvas and silk. You could work

on reproductions. All those immaculate works of art that we

could recreate…" Mr. Shi appeared to wax poetic at the

thought.

Everything that went by in the next few minutes

seemed like a dream to Chang. He was being offered a

contract, worth more than he could dream of, to produce

more and more such beautiful forgeries. Suddenly, all he

cared about was that he had arrived! Years of care, penury

and need seemed to fall away from him like the shedding of a carapace.

He had made it! He was going to be in the multi-billion-dollar mass production industry that typified the success of his milieu, and at the high end of it. He'll never be in need again. Little did he realize though, nor would he have cared, that he had lost the freedom and joy of pure creativity, complete freedom of expression and artistic license that was the hallmark of a true master. He chose to forget and forego the joys and passions that had stirred in him all those weeks during the wonderful days of creating his masterpiece.

*****

6 IVORY

When Jason Krantz arrived in Zambia's Sioma Ngwezi National Park, he had only one objective - Ivory. And, of course, he was looking forward to the thrill of the hunt. It had been decades since big game hunting or poaching was banned in most countries, but that did not matter at all to him.

Krantz was rich. A billionaire. Minor legalities that were designed for the rest of the world did not affect him in the least. He was well aware that laws applied only to the unfortunate lot of the common man, he himself was quite well above it all.

Besides, he was a collector. He was a hunter. He

loved his trophies. He had a Bengal tiger from India, a giraffe and even a snow leopard from Russia. Besides all the bison, moose and elk. These were his private collection and he knew that as long as it stayed private, no one was going to care.

He had found the perfect helper for this particular venture. He was Banji, a tribal officer, who had been recommended to him as someone who can help with elephants. Banji was waiting to greet him. Various amounts of cash had exchanged hands until he got to this point. Now he was ready for the real deal.

Banji said that it was arranged for them to go out the next day into a secure area atop a tree, near where a small herd of elephants were known to frequent. It was actually quite near a tribal settlement. Not exactly in the wild. But he promised that that would work in their favor. Krantz did not quite understand how being closer to a farm would help them. But he had been informed that Banji was the man to trust in this matter, so he acquiesced.

***

Early the next afternoon, they were both riding in a battered jeep, in the general direction of a village on the outskirts of the park.

While driving, Banji detailed the situation of elephants in Zambia, Botswana and other nearby nations. Despite the ban, poaching was a very regular activity. Only more clandestine. The elephants, who usually lived in herds with the oldest female being the leader, were being regularly hunted. Their populations had fallen to single digits in some areas. This, from thousands originally.

Often, the female leaders were killed because their tusks were really long and very valuable. This meant the herds were without a leader and they became smaller and also, instead of a single-family unit, which they traditionally were, they were now mostly a few mixed family stragglers. The nature of the herd had changed. It was quite a dire situation.

Krantz listened to all of this explanation as nothing more than a ploy to make some more money out of him. He was used to these touches, and he merely grunted. He will pay him a little something to make sure he was happy. These things had to stay quiet.

Soon they arrived near the settlement and Banji showed him to a little platform that was raised up on a tree. There was a wooden ladder to climb up. The elephants came this way to eat off the trees and this spot provided a great vantage point. It was not too difficult to shoot one from this height.

Krantz got his elephant gun all checked and ready. It was loaded with cartridges. This was a heavy gun, not something you can carry easily in the wild. He would have needed to hire help for that. As such, Banji had helped and no one else seemed to be involved. Maybe Banji wanted all the money to himself. It was only a few steps from the jeep to the tree.

Little did Krantz know that elephant hunting by

foreigners was despised by the locals. For them, the elephants were auspicious, even sacred animals and only the bad ones like Banji ever willfully destroyed them. They knew that elephants helped the trees by spreading the seeds and facilitated the resilience of the forests. They fertilized the lands. It was not easy to get a large party from among the tribesmen to hunt these gentle giants.

As dusk came, they waited with growing anticipation. It was absolutely beautiful with the fading orange sky as a backdrop to the plains of Africa with just low trees dotted about. The light was almost faded when they heard the familiar, at least to Banji, trumpeting sounds that elephants usually make. They were not loud, more like gentle calls to each other. They were near at hand.

Soon, they were within sight and it was a magnificent view, these large yet graceful animals ambling along, pulling their last bits of food from the trees around them. There was a large female, with three younger ones and two little baby ones. The old female had tusks at least five feet long, Krantz noted with relish.

They were just grazing, pulling at this branch and that leaf, ready for that last bite that will get them to their sleep. Elephants don't sleep too long; they only need a short rest.

As they got closer, Krantz took aim at the female and when she finally looked in their direction, her head all exposed directly to them, he fired.

The large caliber ensured that there was no need for anything else. The animal swayed and in slow motion fell down and lay spread out on her side, quite dead. Banji motioned to Krantz to stay still. He did not understand, but obeyed.

That was when he noticed that the other animals in the herd were standing around the dead female; they raised their trunks and touched her and whinnied softly. When he looked more closely, he saw that they were crying. Actually, crying with tears flowing down from their eyes. He had not known that elephants could cry.

They waited a few hours before the dusk fully fell when the rest of the herd finally started melting away. It was a moving sight. Except for Krantz, who was quite unmovable about such things. Even Banji seemed to be awed at the tenderness and emotion of these gentle creatures.

***

It was all done, Krantz had his ivory and everything was completed satisfactorily to him, at least. Now he understood why Banji came highly recommended. He had arranged the papers. Being next to the human settlement had been a brilliant idea. The reason for killing the elephant had been explained as necessary as they were attacking the settlement. It was not poaching, but self- defense. These elephants occasionally caused havoc with human settlements and then they were justified in taking action. The papers clearly stated that this was justified.

Banji had also ensured that no one else even saw Krantz, although the dismemberment of the animal and removal of ivory had been done with a lot of help from the villagers. He had paid for the arrangements, a tidy sum in Zambia, but hardly a hole in his pocket for all of these arrangements.

When the ivory came, he finally handed over the largest payout. It was a king-sized ransom for Zambian standards, but he knew that was the going rate. The ivory was packed and ready for him at the airport. He had been given the papers showing that this was a legitimate culling and the ivory was legal for export. He only had to pay the export duty now.

And, just like that, the final transaction was concluded and the private collection grew by another forbidden trophy.

*****

7 SOULMATES

It was dusk when the cab pulled up on the side of the street and a man jumped out from the front passenger seat and opened the back door. Without much ceremony, he helped out a bent, wizened looking old woman and led her to the curb. Unceremoniously, he pulled out a bundle of plastic bags and deposited it next to her on the side of the road.

The man who dropped her got back in the car and it drove away. She didn't notice. She didn't really know where she was or what she was supposed to be doing. Confused and disoriented, she merely sat there, looking about her this way and that, trying to make sense of her situation. The place looked vaguely unreal to her, she could not recall having been there before... but these days, she was never very sure of anything. Maybe this was her home?

She sat there immobile, for a long while… night had fallen and she had no idea of the time. Had she eaten? She never seemed to remember even that these days… she had stopped recognizing hunger a long time ago. The dark always confused her more… brought on strange fears and panic. She began to fidget a little, growing restless with the uncertainty of it all.

Just then another cab drove up, parked almost exactly where hers had. With a sense of déjà vu and a cursory interest for want of anything better to do, she watched a man jump out from the front and open the back door. He helped out a limp bundle of rags and led him to a spot a few feet away from her. A similar lump of cloth and plastic was dropped beside him. Without further ado, the man got back in his car and it was gone.

For several minutes nothing stirred among the new arrivals. She glanced that way furtively, every now and then, wary, trying to see what it all was about. Then she thought she heard it. A low moan! Unsure, she strained to hear…

there it was again… a vague memory stirred within her. This must be Mike.

What was Mike doing here? An intense feeling of joy shot through her! Scrambling up, she rushed, with an unexpected burst of speed to his side. Throwing herself beside him, she pulled away the blanket over his face and reached for him in an enveloping embrace.

The man, for indeed it was a man, struggled for an instant and then cried out – "help!" She was overcome with pity and started murmuring soft, comforting sounds, holding him all the while and rocking him back and forth. Presently, he settled down and she started to talk.

"Mike, what took you so long? Where have you been?"

He was confused – "I am Mike? I thought I had another name!"

She cried – "Of course, you are my Mike! Remember, we played together in your house, went swimming in the lake, tried to catch fish with some floss and a blue lure."

"Eh?" He was nonplussed. He couldn't recall any of

those things in his past. But then he could not remember

even his own name these days. Maybe she was right; she

was the one who could help him. He turned in her arms and

faced her. Her eyes looked down on him gently, with all the

love he could ever hope to see in anyone's eyes. He felt

strangely moved. He slowly raised his arm and touched her

face. They stared at each other for a long moment and then

reached for a strong warm embrace.

Soon he felt good enough to sit up and they started to

talk.

She was telling him of summer days when they

played outdoors. How his dad taught them to whittle

whistles. Of how they had had these enormous appetites

and had eaten everything in sight, till his mom had to chase

them out of the kitchen. In his mind, these images started to

take shape and achieve a modicum of reality. Her

enthusiasm and clarity of long-ago memories let his

imagination take flight and he found himself agreeing with

everything she was saying. He could feel the heat of the sun

on his young face as they ran around, the smells of his

mother's cooking. He loved this woman, who was his friend, his lifeline.

Was she his friend? He had to ask. She laughed, cackling gleefully at his folly… "No kiddo!" She said joyously. "I am your cousin, Minnie. They used to call me that those days."

He was not sure he could remember that, but it must be true. She said it with such conviction. She understood him so well. That was a lot more than he could say about himself right then. He vaguely remembered a cigarette in his bundle somewhere. Fiddling around, he finally found it and his book of matches. Cupping it close, he lit up and felt the warmth course through. He passed it to her and soon they were puffing along peacefully.

She continued to ramble about their childhood in vivid detail. Events, sights, sounds, smells… people, places, pets… she was animated in her memories and her realities became his, as he struggled to equate those details with some similar, long forgotten retentions in his own mind.

She pouted, accused him of stealing her comic books,

and laughed as he apologized. She hadn't minded at all. She was just teasing.

They reveled, she, in the return of her childhood and he, in an imagined, superimposed reality that was not his own. They were children again, playful at times, fighting at others, forgetting their annoyances and moving onto more and more shared or make-believe encounters. They hummed a few songs, but they found that their likes did not match. So, they went back to the stories that she, mainly, told.

They were both feeling utterly content, which was something they had not known in a long while. In their minds, there was nothing they needed any longer, nowhere else they needed to be. They were, simply put, totally happy. In their gaiety, awareness suddenly came back to them. They gazed upon their surroundings, noticing the little deli across the road, the gas station all lit up a few yards away. They had seen a man in there talking on his phone and they giggled about who he might be calling this late at night. They said anything that came into their heads and each observation made the other laugh. They were comrades, friends with no demands to make of the other, no requirements except easy company!

A pale dawn was breaking when they heard some wailing sirens and before they knew it, several cars with lights flashing had drawn up to their curbside. Men in uniforms jumped out and came over to them.

One of them said that the gas station attendant had called them, they had been dumped there. What, what? Dumped? Neither of them could comprehend what these people were saying. But the cops were trying to say something to them that they did not want to understand.

One of the officers said "This is Skid Row." What was that? Sounded like a playground of sorts!

Soon it started getting through to them, that they were being taken away. They each had, what was it they were saying, "Alshmers"? They needed help and doctors. They were sick. Some hospitals did not want them and so they had to go somewhere else. Helpless to even protest, they found themselves gently led away to separate cars and as they strained to get a glimpse of each other, were quietly ushered in, into another of the strange unknowns, which was what life for them was in these confusing days.

A fleeting instance of loss was all each felt, for their minds had already forgotten their brief interlude. Still, they departed, the chance encounter having left them both a little happier, like a few drops of rain on otherwise parched earth. Until even that will fade away, eventually, in the confusion that is Alzheimer's disease.

*****

8 THE CASE OF THE WERE-RABBIT

I first met him on an unsuspecting morning, as I was tooling off to work, in a rush as usual. Little did I know how deep and profound our acquaintance was going to be.

I had turned the corner, stopping briefly at the stop sign and noticing no buzz of activity in the almost private road, had turned with the hopes of getting to a decent speed. As I turned, I spied him a few meters away and as I came abreast, he stepped off the curb and leaped at my car. My heart sank, I hit the brakes, jerked to a stop and feeling no impact, I started again, really slowly, this time. There was no sound of crunching bone, no bump in movement to indicate that I had run over him.

I looked in my rear; there was no sign of him, save for a flash of bobtail on the other side of the road.

I have seen birds, squirrels and other creatures, all with a healthy instinct for survival, all leaping away hurriedly at my approach. Even other rabbits did so, with great dispatch. As rabbits go, this one seemed an aberration. Shaking my head, I sped off on my way.

This would have been just a quotidian incident, completely unremarked in my memory, were it not for what was to follow.

Over the next few weeks, I encountered the same little guy around six times and each time, like a thing possessed, he leaped in like fashion, at my wheels. This strange behavior of his, was what made me certain that he was the same little guy every time, for he had no distinguishing marks or other mannerisms that made him discernible in any other way.

Every day, once this had happened more than once, I

approached the spot on the road with trepidation. He always chose the same place to wait for me and always seemed to know that it was me approaching! Each time I saw him, I winced. I approached, gingerly, and tried to shuffle past him in an incognito mode and he seemed to see through me every time. Each time, I hit the brakes and stopped and started and gazed earnestly backwards... Each time, the expected scrunch did not come.

I tried to look at it from his point of view. Maybe he had a death wish; he was born without the survival gene. Maybe it is all a game to him, and he is the Evel Knievel of the rabbit world! Was he doing this to other hapless drivers? Each time I approached the spot, I felt concern and fear and guilt and hesitation... a mixture of umpteen emotions. Did he get some jollies from it all? Can he smell my feelings? Did he have bets with other evil rabbits? Did he do it on a dare? He was a strange little guy and definitely unique enough to make a lasting impression on me. How did he come to the same place at the same time and seem to jump at the same car, with the same reckless unconcern for his life? How can such an insignificant animal make such an impact on another species and inspire such fantastic thoughts and feelings? The non-sequitur did not seem at all ludicrous to my astonished mind, in light of the bizarre behavior of this blob of fur, this kamikaze rabbit.

It has now been a couple of weeks since I last saw him.

As I come to our rendezvous spot each day, I always feel a familiar twinge… but he has remained scarce. I feel a sense of disappointment and relief with each passing day. I know that as long as I drive by his hangout, for a fleeting instant, I am going to recall our puzzling encounters and I will check and stop and start each time, for a long time to come. He is a familiarity and a conditioned reflex. Brief though our tangles, he will forever remain in my psyche. Even if I have to close the file on the Case of the Were-rabbit!

*****

A thought fleeting; gone...

a sudden twinge, was it real?

Sure, there's tomorrow.

ABOUT THE AUTHOR

Rema Nair is a retired microelectronics engineer. She has a Masters in Materials Engineering from the University of Southern California. She has worked for companies such as Hewlett-Packard, Intel, Medtronic and Abbott/St. Jude Medical. However, she has always been interested in creative writing. She believes that imagination gives her wings. She has traveled widely and that informs many of her stories. This collection of short stories was inspired by many people she has met or observed and she has added color and imagination to these casual observations. At the end of the book is a haiku that typifies her outlook on life – there is always tomorrow.

www.ingramcontent.com/pod-product-compliance
Lightning Source LLC
Chambersburg PA
CBHW020545130626
46552CB00007B/2766